W9-AUI-699

# Santa's Winter Vacation

Viveca Lärn Sundvall

Illustrations by Olof Landström

*Translated by Kjersti Board*

Stockholm New York London Adelaide Toronto

Rabén & Sjögren Stockholm


Originally published in Sweden by Rabén & Sjögren
under the title *Ruben,* copyright © 1994 by Viveca Lärn Sundvall
Illustrations © 1994 by Olof Landström
Library of Congress catalog card number: 95-067817
Printed in Hungary
First edition, 1995

ISBN 91 29 62953 5

During the darkest and most depressing part of November, Reuben Stormfoot took a trip with his wife, Hosannah. He didn't bring much - just a green toothbrush and a pair of red swimming trunks. Reuben never shaved; he hadn't shaved in forty-seven years. Hosannah took lots of suitcases filled with gorgeous dresses, gold sandals, and a bit of this and a bit of that.

The plane to Spain was filled with pale and sniffling Swedes going to the Canary Islands to lie in the sun, swim, and run in the sand. Seated in front of Reuben and Hosannah was the Sandworm family from Stockholm. “Check the weird beard on that old guy!” said the oldest boy. He was seven and was called Linus.

"Awesome!" exclaimed his little brother, giggling. He was called Lucas, and was six.
The youngest brother, Johannes, who was four, knelt in his seat and smiled at Reuben. He didn't say anything.
"Be quiet, Johannes!" said the boys' mother. "Soon you'll get something to eat."
Reuben winked at Johannes.

A flight attendant passed out trays with lunch, and everyone got to choose what he or she wanted to drink. No one spilled anything; everybody was happy, and the sky outside was blue. Everyone got little packets of salt and pepper, and Reuben hid his in his beard. Johannes saw him and giggled out loud.

“Be quiet, Johannes,” his father scolded him. “Soon they’ll come around with toys.”

The flight attendant passed out jigsaw puzzles, but there were only two left and she gave them to Linus and Lucas.
"You're probably too little for puzzles anyway," she said kindly to Johannes.
He nodded and played with his napkin.

At the airport in Spain, two customs officials were checking that no one was trying to smuggle anything into the country.

"I think we'll have to go through the beard of that one with a fine-tooth comb," one of them whispered to the other, nodding toward Reuben.

"It has salt and pepper in it," said Johannes.

"Mom, Johannes already has got sunstroke," Linus said.

All kinds of things fell out of Reuben's beard. Then the passport official looked at Reuben's passport.
"A hundred and eighteen years old?" He sniffed. "You expect us to believe that?"
Reuben smiled apologetically.
"I eat a lot of oatmeal," he said. "It keeps me young."

Soon everyone was lying on air mattresses on the Spanish beach. Hosannah and the boys' parents put on some suntan lotion and settled down for several hours, flat as flounders, while Linus and Lucas played with their new polka-dot beach balls. Johannes built a little sand castle at the edge of the water, using a yellow shovel that he found. Reuben was wading around on his long legs, collecting pretty little seashells, which he put in a pail.

"What a nut!" exclaimed Lucas, pointing at Reuben.

"Yeah, wacky!" Linus said.

Reuben gave the seashells to Johannes. He was happy and made a fence around his castle.

In the evenings there was dancing at the hotel, and everybody watched Reuben and Hosannah as they glided around the dance floor. They danced the tango best of all.
"People that old should stay home and play bingo," said the boys' mother, who was envious of Hosannah's silk dresses.
The boys' father shook his head. He only knew how to do a slow dance. Linus and Lucas jumped up onto the dance floor and made fun of Reuben and Hosannah.
"I think they dance nicely," said Johannes. "The man is called Reuben."

After a week, the vacation was over and everyone was sitting in the airplane again. Linus and Lucas had gotten large Spanish straw hats, and Johannes had gotten freckles.
"That's the end of the good life," the boys' mother said to Hosannah. "But when you are retired, I guess you are able to take it easy almost all of the time."

“Definitely not!” said Hosannah. “I supervise a toy workshop and work forty-two hours a week. But it’s true that my husband works only one day a year.”

“Some job!” The boys’ father sniffed.

“Yes, but then I work like a dog.” Reuben smiled and pulled a deck of cards out of his beard and started to show Johannes some magic tricks.

On Christmas Eve, the Sandworms were seated in front of the TV, cracking nuts, like so many other Swedes.

Santa, however, was hard at work. He had put on his red work clothes and was going all around his large district handing out Christmas gifts. He had three gifts left in his bag when he knocked at the Sandworms' front door.

The boys' father filmed Santa with his camcorder as he handed Johannes the first package.

The other boys started to fuss.
“How come he gets the first one? That little pipsqueak!”

Then Santa handed Johannes the other two packages, too.
The living room became absolutely quiet. You could almost hear the needles drop from the Christmas tree.

Johannes chuckled.
“You’re funny, Reuben,” he said, handing the other gifts to his brothers, Linus and Lucas.

Outside in the street, the snow made a crunchy noise under Reuben's boots. The sky was almost black, but the stars were shining and winking at him. Reuben winked back at them. Far away, from the edge of the woods, came a sound of music that made him smile.

Reuben folded up his empty bag and put it on the sled. Then he pushed off toward the tiny gray house which lay almost hidden among the pine trees in the woods. That's where the music was coming from. It was a tango.

Reuben opened the door and recognized the wonderful smells of Christmas that he knew he would never grow tired of, no matter how many hundred years he lived.

Hosannah came dancing toward him. The bells on her silk dress were tinkling.

"How was work this year?" she asked.

"Great," Reuben said. "Especially at Johannes's house."